DC SUPER-PETS!™

Raintree is an imprint of Capstone Global Library Limited, a company incorporated in England and Wales having its registered office at 264 Banbury Road, Oxford, OX2 7DY – Registered company number: 6695582

www.raintree.co.uk
myorders@raintree.co.uk

Designed by Hilary Wacholz
Originated by Capstone Global Library Ltd

978 1 3982 3942 5 (hardback)
978 1 3982 4137 4 (paperback)

British Library Cataloguing in Publication Data
A full catalogue record for this book is available from the British Library.

BEPPO!

The **Origin** of Superman's Monkey

by Steve Korté
illustrated by Art Baltazar
Superman created by Jerry Siegel and Joe Shuster
by special arrangement with the Jerry Siegel family

raintree

a Capstone company — publishers for children

EVERY SUPER HERO NEEDS A
SUPER-PET!

Even Superman! In this
origin story, discover how
Beppo the Super-Monkey
became the Man of Steel's
faithful friend . . .

In a faraway galaxy, a family lives on a planet called Krypton.

Jor-El and Lara are the parents of a baby called **Kal-El**. They also have a pet monkey called **Beppo**, who is always getting into mischief.

Jor-El is a scientist, and he has discovered that Krypton is going to explode. Just minutes before the explosion, Jor-El and Lara place their son inside a rocket ship.

"There isn't room for all of us," says Jor-El. "But we can send Kal-El to the planet Earth, where he will be safe."

"Earth's yellow Sun will give Kal-El amazing powers," says Lara.

But Kal-El won't be alone. When no one is looking, Beppo hops into the ship.

The rocket ship shoots into space! Kal-El and Beppo sleep during the long journey to Earth.

After travelling millions of kilometres, the rocket lands in a dusty field outside the town of **Smallville**.

Jonathan and Martha Kent find Kal-El inside the rocket ship.

The Kents decide to take the boy home to live with them on their farm. They carry Kal-El to their truck and drive away.

After they are gone, Beppo slowly pokes his head outside the rocket ship.

"Uh-oh," he says nervously. "Where is everybody?"

Beppo jumps out of the rocket. To his surprise, he shoots up into the air!

Beppo can suddenly fly!

"**Wheeeee!**" cries the monkey as he flies over the field.

Beppo isn't watching where he is flying. He slams into a tall oak tree.

SMASH!

The impact knocks the tree over. Beppo isn't hurt at all!

Beppo scratches his head. "What's going on?" he wonders. **"Why am I suddenly so strong?"**

Beppo thinks for a moment. "I should try to find Kal-El!" he says.

Beppo starts flying. He heads towards the big city of **Metropolis** in the distance.

"Maybe Kal-El is in that city,"
says Beppo.

Minutes later, Beppo soars over the Metropolis City Zoo. He sees monkeys sitting in a tree and eating bananas.

Beppo lands on the tree and helps himself to a banana. He peels it and swallows it whole.

"Wow!" says Beppo. "That was yummy! I wonder what other tasty treats they have here."

Beppo soon finds the room where all the food for the animals is stored. He gobbles up many more bananas.

"I like this place," he declares. "I think I'll stay here for a while!"

Over the next few days, Beppo wanders around the zoo. He explores the exhibits.

In the reptile house, a crocodile sneaks up on Beppo. The creature opens its mouth wide to bite the monkey!

The crocodile clamps its mouth down.

BOING!

But the reptile's sharp teeth bounce off the monkey's super-strong body.

Beppo is totally unharmed!

Later, Beppo visits the big cat exhibit. When he's not looking, a tiger attacks!

The tiger leaps through the air. It is about to scratch Beppo with its claws!

"Oh no you don't!" shouts the superpowered monkey.

Beppo soars over the charging feline. He grabs the tiger's tail and ties it around a log.

The angry tiger glares at Beppo as the monkey flies away.

Soon, all the other animals in the zoo know not to mess with Beppo.

Back in Smallville, the Kents raise Kal-El as their son. They name him **Clark**.

As he grows up, Clark discovers that he has many **amazing superpowers**.

He can fly, and he has incredible strength.

He can also blow freezing cold winds with his breath and blast red-hot laser beams from his eyes!

When he becomes a young man, Clark decides to use his powers to fight crime. He puts on a blue uniform and a bright red cape.

He becomes **Superman, the Man of Steel!** He is Earth's mightiest Super Hero.

One day, Superman flies over Metropolis. He is rushing to a bank that has just been robbed by the Super-Villain **Lex Luthor**.

As Superman soars above the Metropolis City Zoo, Beppo looks up.

"He has the same powers as me!"

says Beppo. **"That could be Kal-El!"**

Beppo flies up to greet Superman.

The Man of Steel is surprised to see a **flying monkey**. But just then, a police helicopter whizzes past both of them.

The helicopter is chasing Lex Luthor's getaway car.

Superman rushes off to join the chase.
Beppo is right behind him.

"Where are we going? What are we
doing?" Beppo asks.

But the only thing Superman hears

is **"Eek! Eek! Eek!"** He doesn't

understand what Beppo is saying.

Lex Luthor leans out of his car and glares at Superman and the monkey.

"I'll deal with that helicopter first," the villain says.

Luthor points a long metal tube at the helicopter. He pushes a button, and a stream of **sticky glue** shoots out of the device.

SPLAT!

Globs of thick, pink glue stick to the blades of the police helicopter.

WHUB! WHUB! WHUB!

The blades slow down. Then they stop spinning.

The helicopter tumbles towards the ground!

Superman makes a quick decision. **He knows he must save the helicopter pilot**, even if it means that Luthor will get away.

WHOOSH!

The Man of Steel rushes over to the
helicopter and grabs it in mid-air.
He gently lowers it to the ground.

Meanwhile, Beppo chases after Luthor.

The villain points the glue device at the monkey.

But before Luthor can push the button, **Beppo uses his heat vision!** Two rays of heat blast out of Beppo's eyes and hit a front tyre on Luthor's car.

The tyre explodes, and the car skids to a stop.

Lex Luthor hops out of the car and starts running.

WHOOOSH!

Beppo blows out a blast of **freezing super-breath** from his mouth. Luthor is trapped within a thick block of ice.

Superman lands next to Beppo. The superpowered monkey happily jumps into the hero's arms.

Beppo wraps his tail around the Man of Steel. **"Eek! Eek! Eek!"**

The next day, the people of Metropolis look up in the sky.

Flying high above the city are two figures, both dressed in blue uniforms with bright red capes.

Superman has a new crime-fighting friend . . .

Beppo the Super-Monkey!

BEPPO!

REAL NAME:
Beppo

SPECIES:
Super-Monkey

BIRTHPLACE:
Krypton

HEIGHT:
90 centimetres

WEIGHT:
25 kilograms

**Super Hero Owner:
SUPERMAN**

HEAT & X-RAY VISION

SUPER-SMELL
No villain (or banana) can escape this nose.

SUPER-HEARING

SUPER-STRENGTH
For a mini-sized monkey, Beppo has gorilla-sized strength!

FREEZE BREATH
Cools down any heated situation

S-SHIELD

SUPER-SPEED

STRONG TAIL

HERO PET PALS!

COMET

Super Hero Owner:
SUPERGIRL

SUPER-
SQUIRREL

Super Hero Owner:
SUPERBOY

VILLAIN PET FOES!

TITANO

Super-Villain Owner:
LEX LUTHOR

BIZARRO
BEPPO

Super-Villain Owner:
BIZARRO

BEPPO JOKES!

What do you get when two monkeys fight over a banana?
A banana split!

What is a monkey's favourite snack?
Chocolate chimp cookies!

What is a monkey's favourite month?
Ape-ril!

GLOSSARY!

device piece of equipment that does a particular job

exhibit collection of things or animals and information that shows and tells people about a certain subject

feline any animal of the cat family

galaxy group of stars and planets

impact hitting of one thing against another

mischief playful behaviour that may annoy other people

scientist person who studies the world around us

uniform special clothes that members of a group wear

villain evil or bad person

READ THEM ALL!

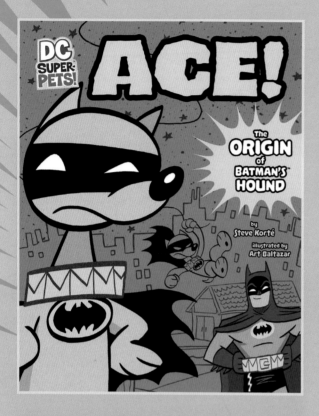

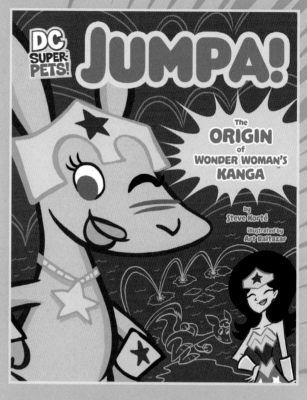

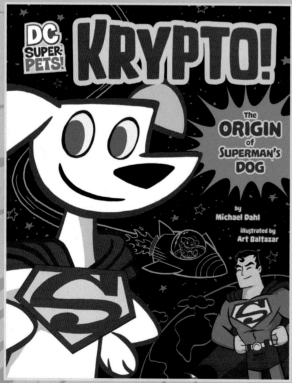

ONLY FROM raintree

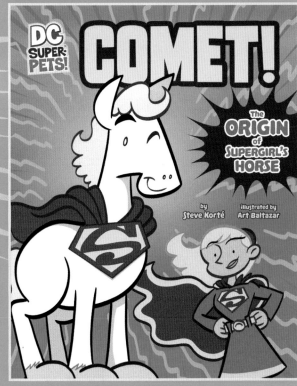

AUTHOR!

Steve Korté is the author of many books for children and young adults. He worked at DC Comics for many years, editing more than 600 books about Superman, Batman, Wonder Woman and the other heroes and villains in the DC Universe. He lives in New York City with his husband, Bill, and their super-cat, Duke.

ILLUSTRATOR!

Famous cartoonist **Art Baltazar** is the creative force behind *The New York Times* best-selling, Eisner Award-winning DC Comics' Tiny Titans; co-writer for Billy Batson and the Magic of Shazam!, Young Justice, Green Lantern: The Animated Series (comic); and artist/co-writer for the awesome Tiny Titans/Little Archie crossover, Superman Family Adventures, Super Powers! and Itty Bitty Hellboy. Art is one of the founders of Aw Yeah Comics comic shop and the ongoing comic series. Aw yeah, living the dream! He stays at home and draws comics and never has to leave the house! He lives with his lovely wife, Rose, sons Sonny and Gordon, and daughter, Audrey! AW YEAH, MAN!